# WHiCH BUM'S MUM'S?

MB — For Sonny and Theo,
who never fail to CRACK me up

Edited by Susannah Bailey
Designed by Jack Clucas
Cover design by John Bigwood

First published in Great Britain in 2022 by Buster Books,
an imprint of Michael O'Mara Books Limited, 9 Lion Yard,
Tremadoc Road, London SW4 7NQ

W www.mombooks.com/buster   F Buster Books   🐦 @BusterBooks   📷 @buster_books

A CIP catalogue record for this book is available from the British Library.

ISBN: 978-1-78055-812-7

1 3 5 7 9 10 8 6 4 2

This book was printed in June 2022 by Leo Paper Products Ltd,
Heshan Astros Printing Limited, Xuantan Temple Industrial Zone,
Gulao Town, Heshan City, Guangdong Province, China.

# WHICH BUM'S MUM'S?

Written by
**JONNY LEIGHTON**

Illustrated by
**MIKE BYRNE**

On a wide savannah, in the blazing summer heat,
Lives the hungriest of zebras that you'd ever hope to meet.
Ziggy munches grasses for his breakfast, lunch and dinner —
He's a **CHOMPING**, **CHEWING**, **GRAZING**, **GUZZLING** all-you-can-eat winner.

Sometimes things are crowded deep inside the zebra herd.
So many stripes of black and white, it's really quite absurd.
Ziggy knows which way to go by keeping Mum's bum near,
With her zig-zag stripes to guide the way, he never has to fear.

Until one day he wanders off and finds a spot to eat,
A patch of grass beneath his feet, "That looks so nice and sweet!"
He takes a bite and to his fright he **CHOMPS** down on a tail
Belonging to a zebra, who starts to **SHOUT** and **WAIL** ...

"DANGER! DANGER! DANGER! A lion bit me, OW!"

"NO!" says Ziggy desperately, "It was me who bit just now..."
But the zebras panic quickly and they set off at top speed,
Before he even knows it, Ziggy's caused a HUGE

# STAMPEDE!

Zebras **DASH**,

flamingos **FLY**

and monkeys take to **TREES.**

Hippos **SPLASH**

and vultures **CRY,**

a meerkat **SQUEAKS** and flees.

Ziggy sadly finds himself a herd of only one.
"I made the zebras scatter and now everyone is gone!
I've got to find my family. I've got to find my home.
It's no good being solo, I don't want to be alone."

He thinks back to the morning as he wandered on the plain.
"As long as I know which bum's Mum's, I'll make it home again!"

At first he finds a stretching bum that's **SMELLY, BIG** and **HAIRY**,
Belonging to a lion who is mighty fierce and scary.

Ziggy asks if Lion's seen the zebras in his herd.
"No, but if you find them let me know," he gently **PURRS**.

Then down by the river there's a bum that's **SMOOTH** and **LARGE**.
It's a hungry-looking hippo who is just about to charge.
"Have you seen my family cross the water?" Ziggy asks.
"No! I'm far too busy," says the hippo **SPLASHING** past.

Reaching for the leaves he sees a bum that's **THIN** and **TALL**.
Compared to this giraffe, Ziggy's mum's is rather small.

"You must have seen my family with your head so **VERY HIGH**."

"I haven't seen a thing, dear boy, now give these leaves a try!"

Ziggy marches forwards on his homeward-bound bum quest.
"There are wrong bums nearly everywhere, it's making me quite stressed."

There are **SPOTTY** bums and **SCALY** bums and bums that slither by.
**FLUFFY** bums and **FEATHERED** bums and bums that cannot fly.

Bums that **JUMP**

and bums with **BUMPS**

and bums covered in **SPOTS**.

Bums that
GROWL

and bums that
HOWL

Bums that

and bums all tied in
KNOTS.

Ziggy's full of worry. "There are just too many types!
The bum that I am looking for has lots and lots of ...

STRIPES!

Ziggy dives into the herd to find the bum he needs,
He sees busy bums and barging bums and bums moving at top speed.
But then he gets distracted by a **RUMBLING** in his tummy,
And spots a patch of grass that looks as if it could be yummy...

"Ziggy, where'd you get to? I've been looking everywhere!"

"MUM, YOU FOUND ME!" Ziggy shouts. "I was coming home, I swear.
I got caught up in all the rush ... the herd was miles away ..."